# FERRET FUN

*Books in the Animal Ark Pets series*

BEN M. BAGLIO

# FERRET FUN

Illustrations by
Paul Howard

Cover Illustration by
Chris Chapman

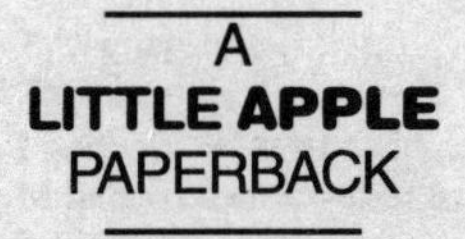


SCHOLASTIC INC.
New York Toronto London Auckland Sydney
Mexico City New Delhi Hong Kong

ISBN 0-439-23023-3



12 11 10 9 8 7 6 5 4 3 2 3 4 5/0

Printed in the U.S.A. 40
First Scholastic printing, December 2000

**Special thanks to Sue Welford**

# *Contents*

# Ferret Fun

# 1

# *Blackie Goes Hunting*

"Hi, Mom! Guess what? We're having a book fair at school!" Mandy Hope didn't stop for breath as she climbed into her mom's Land Rover.

"A book fair?" Dr. Emily Hope started the engine and pulled out from the long line of cars outside the school gates.

"Yes," Mandy said. "Someone's bringing in a whole lot of books, and we can choose which ones we want for the school library. *And* we can buy some to take home if we like."

"That sounds fun." Mandy's mom drove along the village main street and turned into the road that led to the old stone house where they lived. Farther along, workmen were laying new pipes, and there was an enormous hole in the road.

"I'll be glad when this work's finished," Dr. Emily commented. "They've had a road drill going all day today, and it's been upsetting some of the animals. One poor dog has been howling nonstop." Mandy's parents were both vets in Welford. Their house was attached to the clinic, which was called Animal Ark.

"Oh, dear," Mandy said. "Poor thing."

"Poor *me,*" her mom said, with a chuckle.

"I hope there are lots of animal books." Mandy was still thinking about the book fair. She loved animals more than anything else in the world and thought about them most of the time.

Dr. Emily smiled. "I expect there will be."

"By the way, we've got a new boy in our class." As usual Mandy was anxious to tell her mom *all* the day's news. "He comes from America and he's got a sister called Leanne, but she's too young to go to school yet."

"America?" Dr. Emily seemed surprised. "So what are they doing in Welford?"

"Their dad's working in Walton for a while," Mandy explained. Walton was their nearest town. They pulled up outside the front gate. "He's staying in one of the houses behind the Fox and Goose," Mandy continued as she got out and ran indoors. The Fox and Goose was the pub at the end of the main street.

"What's the hurry, Mandy?" Dr. Emily asked, following her daughter into the kitchen.

"James is coming over. We're taking Blackie for a walk." Mandy dumped her schoolbag on the table and went to the cupboard for a bag of chips. James Hunter was her best friend. He was a year younger than she and loved animals almost as much as she did. He had two pets —

a Labrador puppy called Blackie and a cat called Benji. "He's bringing Danny," Mandy went on, munching her chips.

"Danny?" Dr. Emily looked puzzled.

"Yes," Mandy said. "Danny Santana. The boy from America."

"Oh, I see," her mom replied. "Are you going to show him around Welford?"

"Yes. I thought we'd start by taking him to see Grandma and Grandpa."

Mandy's mom gave her a quick hug. "That's kind of you, love. I'm sure they'll be pleased to meet him."

Mandy grinned. "I hope so." She finished her chips and went upstairs to change out of her school clothes. She had just come down when there was a knock at the back door. When she opened it, James was standing there with Blackie and Danny. Danny was taller than Mandy. He had a round face, his dark hair was cut very short, and he was wearing jeans. His baseball cap was on backward.

"Hi, James! Hi, Danny! Hi, Blackie!"

Blackie jumped up as Mandy bent down to hug him. He licked her face all over.

"He's great, isn't he?" Danny said. "He licked me, too."

"He licks everybody," James said. "The milkman, the postman. He even licks Mrs. Ponsonby."

Danny looked puzzled. "Who's she?"

Mandy explained about bossy Mrs. Ponsonby, who lived in a big house called Bleakfell Hall just outside Welford. "She's got a Pekingese called Pandora," she told him.

Mandy took them inside and introduced Danny to her mom.

"I hope you'll enjoy living in Welford," Dr. Emily said to him.

"I like it already," he said, "although it's kind of small. My sister doesn't like it very much, though."

"Why not?" Mandy couldn't imagine anyone *not* liking Welford.

Danny shrugged. "I guess she misses her friends."

Dr. Emily smiled. "I'm sure she'll soon make

new ones. Everyone here knows everyone else, so that makes it a really nice place to live."

"I suppose so." Danny shrugged again and gave a sigh. Mandy realized he was probably missing *his* friends, too.

"How old is your sister?" Dr. Emily asked.

"She's four and a half." Danny made a face. "And she's a pest."

Dr. Emily smiled again. "Oh, I'm sure that's not true."

Danny grinned. "She's okay. She's just being naughty because she's lonely, I guess. Mom says she'll make new friends soon and settle down."

"I'm sure she will," Dr. Emily said.

"Shall we go and see Grandma and Grandpa now?" Mandy suggested.

"Yes, please!" James's face lit up. He loved visiting Mandy's grandparents — there was usually homemade lemonade and freshly baked cakes waiting for them!

Blackie tugged at his leash as they shut the gate behind them. They began to make their way along the road to Lilac Cottage, where Grandma and Grandpa lived.

At the end of the road, Blackie stopped to say hello to the workmen. James had to drag him away as he tried to peer into the hole in the road.

"That dog would make friends with anyone," Danny said. He laughed as James had trouble dragging his puppy away.

When they arrived at Lilac Cottage, Grandma was in the kitchen but there was no sign of Grandpa. Mandy introduced Danny.

"Hi, Danny." Grandma shook his hand. "Where do you come from in America?"

"California." Danny eyed the tray of newly baked chocolate cookies that she had just taken out of the oven. "My grandma bakes a lot, too," he added in a wistful voice.

"That's nice," Grandma said. "Now, sit down, all of you, and I'll fetch some lemonade to go with these cookies."

"Wow, thanks!" Danny sat down at the table with Mandy and James. Blackie was sniffing the air. He could smell the cookies, too.

"Behave yourself, Blackie," Grandma warned, "or I'll tie you up outside."

Blackie cocked his head to one side at the sound of his name.

Danny laughed. "Does Blackie like chocolate cookies as well?"

"He likes anything," Grandma replied. She patted his silky head. "Don't you, Blackie? But chocolate isn't good for dogs." She went to the fridge and brought out a large bone wrapped in brown paper. "I got this from the butcher specially for you, Blackie." Blackie looked very excited. "Is it all right if he has this?" Grandma asked James. She often had a bone ready for when Blackie came to visit.

James was still staring at the cookies. "Er . . . oh, yes, of course."

"I'll take him outside," Mandy offered. "He'll probably make a mess on the floor with it."

"Good girl," Grandma said. "Grandpa's out there, somewhere — he'll keep an eye on him."

Mandy took the bone and went out into the garden. Blackie followed eagerly, his tail wagging so fast it was just a blur. But then, instead of jumping up for the bone, Blackie suddenly stopped. He sniffed the air and gave a little whine. Mandy frowned. What on earth was the matter?

The puppy took off like a rocket. He ran all around the lawn and ended up close to the garden shed. Then he barked loudly and began to sniff the ground. He disappeared around the back of the shed. Suddenly showers of earth flew into the air as he began to dig frantically.

Mandy heard a shout and Grandpa came out of the shed. "Hey, what's going on?" Then he saw Mandy. "Hello, love, I didn't know you were here. What on earth's wrong with Blackie?"

"I don't know." Mandy ran to drag him away. "Blackie! Stop it, for goodness' sake!" She grabbed his collar and pulled him back.

"What *has* he found?" Grandpa asked as he helped Mandy. Although Blackie was only a puppy, he was very strong.

Grandpa bent and peered under the shed. "There must be something under there."

Mandy mentioned how Blackie had left his bone to go sniffing.

"Well!" Grandpa stood up. "It must be pretty exciting if it's better than a bone."

They dragged Blackie back to the lawn. But as soon as they let him go he ran off again, around the back of the shed, sniffing and whining.

Grandma, James, and Danny came out to see what all the fuss was about. Danny went off to investigate.

"It's probably a mouse," Grandpa said. "I heard something scrabbling around this morning when I was sorting out my flowerpots."

Danny was on his hands and knees trying to look under the shed. "There *is* something there. I can see it."

Suddenly Grandma gave a squeal. "Oh, dear! It's a rat, I just saw its nose."

As she spoke, a tiny pink pointed nose popped out. Then it disappeared again.

Mandy took a step backward. She loved *pet* rats, but she wasn't so sure about wild ones.

Danny had put his hand under the shed.

"Be careful!" Grandpa warned him.

Danny was grinning. "Don't worry," he said, putting his arm farther in. "I know what it is." Then, to everyone's surprise, he brought out a small, slim animal. It squirmed in Danny's hands as he lifted it up for everyone to see.

Mandy could hardly believe her eyes. "Oh!" she breathed. "It's a ferret."

Danny stood up, the furry, honey-colored creature held close to his chest. He stroked it gently with his other hand. "It's only a young one," he told them.

Grandpa came closer. "How on earth did it get under my shed?"

"I bet it's escaped from its cage," Danny said. "I've got some ferrets at home in America. They sometimes get out if I'm not careful."

James came across to see the ferret. He had tied Blackie up, to keep him out of mischief.

"Careful," Grandpa warned again, as this time Mandy stretched out her hand to stroke it. "Ferrets can give a nasty bite."

"Only if they're really scared and haven't been petted much," Danny explained, still stroking the ferret gently. It lay still and relaxed in his arms. "This one's really cute."

Mandy touched the tiny head warily. Then, when she saw the creature was quite happy

nestling up against Danny's shirt, she stroked its soft fur. The ferret gazed at her with tiny, sparkling, dark eyes. It was about the size of a small rabbit but much thinner, with short legs and dainty feet, a slender furry tail, pointed pink nose, and perky ears.

Even though the ferret's fur was a bit ragged and dirty from being under Grandpa's shed, Mandy was enchanted by the little creature.

"I wonder where it came from." James looked at Grandpa. "Do you know anyone who keeps ferrets, Mr. Hope?"

Grandpa shook his head. "No one around here that I know of," he told them. "There used to be people who kept them years ago, but I don't know of anyone now." Grandpa had lived in Welford all his life.

"It's really skinny," Danny said. "I think it's been lost for some time."

"Poor thing," Mandy murmured. Her heart turned over as she looked up at her grandpa. "What shall we do with it, Grandpa?"

Grandpa tipped his cap to the back of his head. "Well, love," he said thoughtfully, "I think the first thing is to take it to Animal Ark for a checkup. And it looks like it needs a good meal."

"What do ferrets eat?" Grandma asked Danny.

"Mine have special dry ferret food," Danny told her. "But they'll eat chopped meat."

"I've got just the thing, then," Grandma said. "It's a good thing I went to the butcher's this morning."

They all followed Danny as he carried the little ferret carefully into the kitchen. Grandma shut all the doors so it couldn't escape. Danny put it down on the floor gently while Grandma got some chopped beef from the fridge. She put some in a small dish.

Mandy, James, and Danny sat cross-legged in a circle on the floor watching the little animal. It stared at them all in turn with its bright little eyes. Then it ran around sniffing. It came over to Mandy and put its tiny front paws on her leg and gazed up at her.

"Oh!" She drew in her breath. "It's so sweet."

"I expect the poor creature would like a drink of water, too," Grandpa said. He fetched a saucer of water and the ferret drank thirstily.

"Poor thing," James said softly.

As Grandma bent down to give the ferret the dish of meat she wrinkled up her nose. "It smells a bit," she said.

"So would *you* if you'd been living under an old shed," Mandy said indignantly. She had already fallen in love with the ferret and didn't want to hurt its feelings.

"They *are* a bit smelly," Danny admitted. "But they can't help it and you soon get used to it."

Mandy didn't care a bit about the ferret being smelly. It was the sweetest thing she had ever seen. She watched as its tiny tongue flicked out to lick the last of the meat from around its mouth. "We'd better take it along to see Mom or Dad now," she said as the ferret lapped the last of the water from the dish.

"Yes," Grandpa said. "It needs a bath, too, by the look of it."

"We can do that at home," Mandy told him.

"You'll need something to carry it in," Grandpa said. "It might jump out of Danny's arms and get lost again."

"That's true," Mandy said. "Have you got a box, Grandma?"

Grandma looked thoughtful, then her face brightened and she disappeared out the door. She came back a minute later with a shoe box in her hand. "I bought some new shoes in Walton a few days ago and haven't got around to throwing this away."

"Just the thing." Grandpa took his gardening penknife and a length of string out of his pocket. He made some holes at each end of the box so air could get inside and handed the string to Grandma.

Grandma fetched an old dish towel and put it in the bottom of the box. "There you are," she said. "A nice cozy little bed for the journey to Animal Ark."

Grandma tied the string securely around the box, then Mandy clapped her hands together. "That's great! Thanks, Grandma, Grandpa. Come on, you two," she said to James and Danny. "Let's go!"

# 2

# *A Checkup*

As soon as Danny put the little ferret into the box it curled up and went to sleep.

"How many have you got at home?" James asked Danny. They had fetched Blackie and were on their way to the clinic.

"Four." Danny was carrying the box carefully tucked under his arm.

"Four!" Mandy exclaimed. "Wow! What are their names?"

"Well," Danny said. "There's Minnie and Judy. They're jills."

James screwed up his nose. "Jills?"

"A jill is a girl ferret," Danny explained.

"Is a boy ferret a jack, then?" Mandy asked.

Danny chuckled and shook his head. "No, a boy is called a hob."

James looked a bit puzzled. "A hob? What are your others called?"

"Bert and Ernie," Danny said. "They're hobs. They're a pale honey color with pink eyes and noses just like this one." He took the box from under his arm and tried to peep through the holes to see if the ferret was all right. Then he looked back at Mandy and James with sad eyes. "I really miss mine," he said. "But my uncle's looking after them, so I'm sure they're okay."

"I expect they're missing you, too," Mandy said.

"I think we should call this one Freddie," James piped up suddenly.

"Freddie Ferret," Mandy grinned at her friend. "That's a great name, James! That is, if it's a hob, of course."

Mandy spotted an old man coming up the road. "Hi, Mr. Bell," she called. Ernie Bell was one of Grandpa's friends and lived in the same row of houses as Danny's family. He had been the village carpenter before he'd retired.

Mr. Bell stared at the box Danny was carrying. "What have you got in there, lad?"

He raised his eyebrows when Danny told him.

"We found it under Grandpa's shed," Mandy added.

"A ferret, eh?" Mr. Bell said in his gruff voice. "What was it doing under Tom's shed?"

"Hiding from Blackie," James explained, with a smile.

"Humph," Mr. Bell didn't seem to think it was very amusing. "What are you going to do with a stray ferret?" he asked.

“We’re getting Mom or Dad to check it over,” Mandy explained patiently.

“Then what?” Mr. Bell asked.

Mandy shrugged. “We’re not sure, are we?” She looked at the others and they both shook their heads.

“Ferrets, whatever next? . . .” Mr. Bell went off down the street, mumbling to himself.

When he had gone, Mandy bit her lip. What *were* they going to do with the ferret once it had been checked? Her heart turned over. She knew her mom and dad were too busy looking after other people's animals to let her keep a pet of her own. Danny wasn't staying in Welford for long, and it probably wasn't a good idea to ask James's mom and dad. Blackie's games might be a bit rough for the little creature, and Benji, the cat, might not like the ferret at all.

When they reached Animal Ark, there were several people and their pets waiting to see Mandy's parents. The three children waited by the desk to tell Jean Knox, the receptionist, that they were there.

"We'll have to try to find his real owner." James had been thinking about Freddie, too.

"Find whose real owner?" Jean came out from the back room.

"This ferret's," Mandy explained.

Danny carefully undid the string around the shoe box and lifted one corner of the lid to show Mrs. Knox.

Jean put on the glasses dangling from a chain around her neck and peeped in. "Oh!" she exclaimed. "Isn't it sweet?" She looked at Danny. "And you don't know who it belongs to?"

Danny shook his head and explained where they had found Freddie.

"We'd like Mom or Dad to check that it's all right," Mandy added.

"Well, you shouldn't have to wait long," Jean told them.

They sat down next to Mrs. Edwards from the grocer's. She was waiting with Tilly, her corgi, who had come for her yearly vaccination.

"You don't know who it might belong to, I suppose?" Mandy asked Mrs. Edwards, once she had taken a peep at Freddie.

The woman shook her head. "No idea," she said. "But someone will be missing it, that's for sure."

It wasn't long before their turn came. Mandy, James, and Danny hurried through the waiting room door with Freddie.

In the examining room, Simon the veterinary nurse was tidying up after the previous patient. He looked surprised when the three friends and Blackie trooped through from the waiting room.

"Hi," he said. Then he spotted the box. "What have you got there?"

Mandy introduced Danny, who then opened the box to show Simon what was inside.

"Wow!" Simon exclaimed. "Is he yours, Danny?"

Danny explained.

". . . and we want to ask Dad to look at him," Mandy added.

"Take a look at who?" Dr. Adam Hope came into the room.

"Freddie," Mandy said as her dad gazed into the box. "Isn't he gorgeous?"

"Freddie, eh?" Dr. Adam put on a glove and took Freddie gently from the box. The ferret was still sleepy and hardly opened its eyes as Dr. Adam examined it.

"He doesn't bite," Danny assured him. "We've been cuddling him for ages."

Dr. Adam turned the ferret over. It had a little clump of white fur under its tummy. "Cuddling *her,*" Mandy's dad corrected him. "Your Freddie is a jill."

"Oh?" Mandy said. Then she smiled. "We can still call her Freddie, though. I'm sure she won't mind."

"Freddie it is, then." Dr. Adam quickly examined the little creature. She sat quietly while he lifted her dainty paws one by one and examined her claws.

"Is she all right?" Mandy asked anxiously. "She was very hungry, so we fed her some of Grandma's meat."

"Only a little bit, I hope," her dad said. "When animals haven't eaten properly for some time, a big meal can upset their tummies."

"It *was* only a little bit," Danny told him. "I knew what to give her, because I've got four ferrets back home in the States."

"You must be an expert then, Danny." Dr. Adam put Freddie down on the examining table. "Well, I'm pleased to tell you she seems fine. She's very tired and has obviously been a stray for some time. Apart from a few fleas that we can soon get rid of, there's nothing that a bath, a good rest, and regular meals won't fix."

"That's great." Mandy heaved a huge sigh of relief.

"I'll give her an injection against distemper, just in case she hasn't already had one." Her dad took a little bottle of clear liquid from the medicine cupboard and filled a syringe. "It's a disease that dogs can catch, but if a ferret gets it, it's usually fatal," he explained.

"Mine have shots every year," Danny told them.

"That's good," Dr. Adam said. He rubbed the place where he had given Freddie her injection.

"Have you got any idea where she might have come from?" Simon asked.

Dr. Adam shook his head. "No idea. Ferrets can travel a long way. She could have come from anywhere."

"Someone will be really worried about her," Mandy said anxiously.

Her dad agreed. "We should try to find her owner. Meanwhile, though . . ." He gazed at Mandy. "I'm afraid we can't keep her here for long. You know the rules about having pets."

Mandy bit her lip. "Yes, I know, Dad, but —"

"I'd really like to look after her," Danny said. "If my mom and dad say it's okay."

Dr. Adam patted Danny's shoulder. "Good idea, Danny," he said. "Especially since you know all about ferrets. Why don't you go home and ask them? If they say yes, I'm sure we can keep Freddie here until you find a cage for her." He picked Freddie up and carried her out to the residential unit at the back of the examining room.

"How many residents are we expecting?" Dr. Adam asked Simon.

Simon looked at the book on the table. "Two cats for operations tomorrow," he said. "And Mike Jordan's Annie is coming in for a few days."

Mandy knew Annie, the little dachshund-terrier cross. Her owner, Mike Jordan, had moved to Meadow Lane some time ago.

"Annie!" she exclaimed anxiously. "What's wrong with her?"

Her dad grinned. "Nothing," he said. "Mike's got to go away on urgent business, and Annie's puppies are due soon. I promised him I'd keep an eye on her while he's away."

"Puppies!" Mandy shrieked. "I didn't know she was going to have puppies!"

Dr. Adam grinned again. "Well, she is, and if you're lucky she might have them here."

Mandy's eyes shone. "That would be great! I could help look after them."

Simon had covered the bottom of one of the wire cages with clean newspaper and sweet-smelling hay and filled the water bowl with fresh water.

"Right," Dr. Adam said. "Let's give her a bath first, shall we?" Simon held Freddie while Mandy's dad went to the sink and filled it with warm water. He took a bottle of flea shampoo from the cupboard above the sink. Freddie didn't mind a bit as Simon lowered her carefully into the water.

"Can I help?" Mandy asked.

"Yes," her dad said. "Put a dab of shampoo on her back and I'll rub it in."

When Freddie had been washed, rinsed, and dried gently with a towel, Danny brushed her fur until it shone. She loved all the attention she was getting and rolled on her back just so her tummy could be brushed. She made little *tick-tick* noises in her throat as they made a fuss over her.

Dr. Adam dusted Freddie with flea powder,

then put her back into her cage. "She looks much better now," he said with a smile.

Danny was hovering impatiently by the door. "Come on, you two," he said to Mandy and James. "Let's go and ask Mom if I can look after Freddie until we find her real owner!"

# 3

# *A New Home*

They soon reached the house where Danny and his family were staying. Danny's little sister, Leanne, was sitting in front of the TV in the living room, sucking her thumb.

Danny introduced Mandy, James, and Blackie to his mother. Blackie trotted through into the front room to see Leanne while they told Mrs.

Santana about the ferret. She looked a bit doubtful when Danny asked if he could look after Freddie.

"Well, honey, I'm not sure," she said. "What will we keep her in?"

"I could make a cage," Danny insisted.

"And we'll help him, won't we, James?" Mandy said quickly.

"Of course we will," James confirmed.

Mrs. Santana still didn't look very certain. "What will happen to her when we go back home?"

"I'm sure her real owner will have turned up by then," Mandy said confidently.

Mrs. Santana smiled. "Well . . . okay, then," she said. "But I don't know where we can get wood to make the cage."

Mandy looked thoughtful, then she suddenly had an idea. She knew Ernie Bell had been doing odd carpentry jobs for Della Skilton at Westmoor House, the old people's home. Maybe he would make a cage for Freddie. She told the others her idea.

"That grumpy old man in the house two doors down?" Mrs. Santana looked doubtful all over again. "He hardly even speaks to me. I don't think *he'd* want to help."

"Oh, he's quite nice, really," Mandy told her. "And my grandma says there's never any harm in asking."

Mrs. Santana smiled again. "Well, okay, but I'd better come with you."

She went into the front room to fetch Danny's sister. Leanne was sitting on the floor with one arm around Blackie. He seemed to be enjoying the TV cartoon, too.

"Come on, honey," Danny's mom said. "We're going to pay a visit to one of our neighbors."

Leanne frowned and clutched Blackie tighter. "Can't I stay here with the puppy?" she pleaded.

"You can bring him with you," her mom said.

"His name's Blackie," James told Leanne.

The little girl's face lit up. "Okay. Come on, Blackie." She got up and held on to Blackie's collar. "He's my friend," she said to Mandy and James as they went outside.

"He's everyone's friend," James told her.

Leanne looked sad. "Can he be my special friend? I don't know anyone here."

"Of course," Mandy said. She felt sorry for the little girl. "If James doesn't mind," she added.

"Not at all," James said.

Danny was frowning. "But he's not your dog, Leanne," he said. He turned to the others. "My dad says she's too young to have a pet of her own yet."

"I'm going to have a kitten when we get back home," Leanne piped up. "Mom promised. Didn't you, Mom?"

"That's right," Mrs. Santana confirmed. She turned to Mandy. "Leanne misses her buddies at play group," she explained.

"I'm sure she does." Mandy thought how difficult it must be, leaving all your friends and not seeing them for ages.

Leanne held Blackie's leash as they made their way along to Mr. Bell's house and knocked on the front door. When there was no answer, Mandy ran around the back to see if he was in the garden. The others followed. Leanne hung on tight to Blackie's leash as he tried to catch up with Mandy.

Mr. Bell was weeding his vegetable garden. There were neat rows of carrots, cabbages, peas, and beans. Stacked up against his greenhouse was a pile of wooden boxes. Mandy eyed them excitedly, hoping they wouldn't have too much trouble persuading Mr. Bell to help them.

Before Mandy could ask him, Danny's mom spotted all the neat rows of vegetables and admired them in a very loud voice.

"Mr. Bell!" she exclaimed. "Those vegetables of yours look wonderful. How do you keep your garden so neat?"

Before they knew it, Mr. Bell had taken Mrs. Santana up the garden path to show her his vegetables.

Mandy, James, Danny, and Leanne waited patiently. Soon, Mr. Bell and Danny's mom came back. Mrs. Santana was smiling.

"Mr. Bell has promised me some of his peas when they're ready to pick," she said. "I bet

they're going to be just the most delicious things we've ever tasted."

"Did you ask Mr. Bell about the cage?" Mandy asked Mrs. Santana.

"Cage?" Ernie frowned. "What cage is that?"

Mandy explained quickly. "Any one of those boxes would do," she said, pointing to the pile by the shed.

Mr. Bell ran his hand around his face. "I need those boxes for my vegetables," he said.

"Couldn't you spare just one? Please?" Mandy asked.

Mr. Bell looked thoughtful. Then he said, "Oh, well, I suppose I could make a cage for that pet of yours. . . . Mind you, she'll need a run as well."

"And tunnels," Danny blurted out.

"Tunnels?" Mr. Bell looked puzzled.

Danny explained how ferrets belonged to the polecat family. In the wild, they lived and hunted in tunnels under the ground. "And they love to play in them," Danny added. "They pop in and out and have great fun. Mine at home have a big run in our backyard. Dad made them some tunnels, didn't he, Mom?"

"That's right," Mrs. Santana confirmed. "But we can't go digging tunnels here, honey. The house doesn't belong to us."

Danny bit his lip. "No," he agreed. "I guess not."

Mandy was listening anxiously. Everyone was quiet for a minute or two as they racked their brains.

Then James came up with an idea.

"I know," he said suddenly. "Water pipes."

Everyone stared at him. "Water pipes?" Mrs. Santana repeated.

"Yes," James's eyes were shining. "We could ask those men digging up the road outside Mandy's house if we could have one of the old ones."

Danny grinned. "Hey, James, that's a great idea."

Even Mr. Bell was nearly smiling. "Right," he said. "You get the pipe and I'll make the cage and the run."

"Oh, thanks, Mr. Bell!" Mandy exclaimed. "I'll ask them when they come back in the morning."

As they ran around the side of the house and out the gate, Mandy heard Mr. Bell asking Danny's mom if she'd like a cup of tea. She chuckled to herself. Mr. Bell wasn't at all grumpy once you got to know him. *Especially* if you admired his vegetable garden!

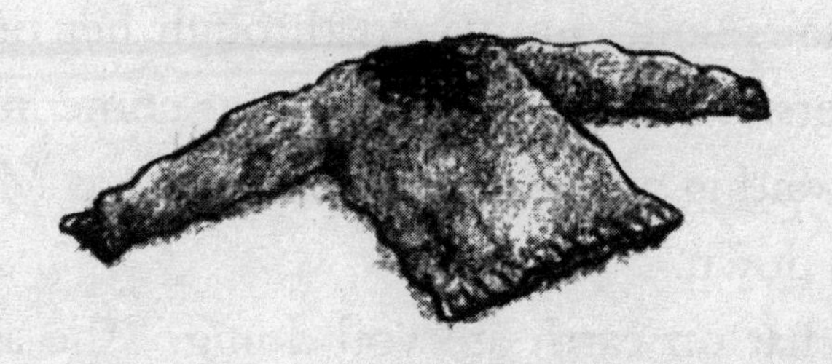

# 4

# *A Problem*

There was just time to visit Freddie before supper, so James and Danny went back to the clinic with Mandy. The little ferret was still curled up, fast asleep.

"She really needs something to burrow into," Danny said, peering through the bars of the cage. "Ferrets love hiding in things."

"What kind of things?" James asked curiously.

"Mine have one of my mom's old sweaters to snuggle in," Danny told them. "They love it."

"*I* know . . ." Mandy ran into the house, up the stairs, and rummaged through her dresser drawers. Dr. Emily had heard her come in. She was waiting at the foot of the stairs as Mandy came down.

"What on earth are you doing?" she asked.

"I've got a sweater for Freddie." Mandy held up a bright pink sweater that Grandma had knitted for her. "I've outgrown it. Do you think Grandma would mind if I gave it to her?"

Dr. Emily laughed and gave Mandy a hug. She had already heard about the stray ferret and had popped in to take a look at her when all the other patients had gone. "Is she feeling cold, then?" she asked.

Mandy laughed as well and told her what Danny had said.

"Well, I'm sure Grandma won't mind a bit," Dr. Emily told her.

"Will this do?" Mandy asked Danny, waving the pink sweater as she came back into the clinic.

"It's great!" Danny took the sweater, opened the cage door, and put it inside. Freddie stirred a bit. She lifted her head and gazed at Danny and the others. Then she gave a yawn, showing her rows of tiny, very sharp teeth. She burrowed into the sweater, curled up, and went to sleep again.

Danny glanced at his watch. "I'd better get back for my supper," he said.

"Me, too," James said. "Mom will be wondering where I am."

Mandy suddenly realized she was hungry as well. So many exciting things had happened in the last few hours that she had completely forgotten the time.

"Shall we ask around the village tomorrow to see if anyone knows who might have lost a ferret?" Mandy suggested as she went to the door with James and Danny. Tomorrow was Saturday.

"Good idea," James agreed. "And we'll ask about the water pipes, too. See you first thing."

Mandy could hardly sleep that night for thinking about the little ferret. She wondered if Freddie was missing her real home. Maybe something had scared her to make her run away. She might have brothers and sisters or other friends to play with. Mandy realized that Freddie could well be feeling lonely, just like Danny's little sister.

Early next morning, as soon as she'd had breakfast, Mandy went through to the back of the clinic to see Freddie. Mike Jordan's little dog, Annie, had arrived. She was curled up in her basket, fast asleep. She got up and stretched and yawned as Mandy came through. Mandy bent down to stroke her.

"How is she?" she asked Simon.

"Fine," Simon said. "I don't think it will be long before her puppies are born."

Mandy's heart leaped with excitement. It would be great if the puppies were born at Animal Ark.

When she had helped Simon feed Freddie, Mandy went outside to see the workmen.

The foreman, whose name was Patrick, grinned when she told him what she wanted.

"Ferret, eh?" he said. "You can have one of those old pipes. They're a bit cracked and broken, but I don't suppose your ferret will mind."

Mandy picked out a length of pipe and washed it carefully under the garden tap before taking it indoors.

Dr. Adam was in the kitchen having breakfast. He looked a bit startled when Mandy appeared with a broken water pipe under her arm.

"It's for Freddie to play in." She explained where it had come from.

Her dad grinned. "That should be fun, Mandy. I'm sure she'll love it."

When James and Danny turned up, she showed them the pipe as well.

"That's fantastic," Danny said. "Can we go and see Freddie now, please?"

"Go ahead," Dr. Adam said.

Mandy took them through to the back. Freddie had now finished her breakfast and was running around in her cage. She looked much better than when they had found her. Although she was still too thin, her fur was sleek and shiny and she was bouncing with energy. They laughed as they watched her burrowing in the sleeve of Mandy's old sweater, peeping

out at them from behind the collar. Mandy hadn't realized ferrets could be quite so much fun.

Dr. Adam let them take Freddie out of her cage, and they sat on the floor while she played around them. She made a little *tick-ticking* sound of pleasure in her throat as she ran around exploring.

"They like balls, too," Danny told them. "And mine have an old sock with a bell tied up in it. They think it's great."

"I bet," Mandy said.

Outside, they could hear Blackie barking. James had tied him up to the gate, and he was anxious for his walk.

"Come on," James said. "We'll take Blackie around the village and ask if anyone knows who's lost a ferret."

"Good idea," Dr. Adam said. "And you can put up a notice in the Animal Ark waiting room so all our patients' owners see it. I'm sure someone will claim her."

⋆ ⋆ ⋆

Although Mandy, James, and Danny asked lots of people in the village, nobody knew anyone who kept ferrets.

By the time they got back to Animal Ark, Mandy felt worried. What would happen if no one turned up to claim Freddie before Danny and his family had to go back to America?

As they trooped through the kitchen door Dr. Emily came in from the clinic. She had a message from Mrs. Santana.

"She just phoned to say that Mr. Bell has arrived with Freddie's cage," she told them. "It's time for her to move." She gave them a pet carrier box to put the ferret in.

When they arrived at Danny's house, the new cage was ready and waiting on the lawn. Leanne had placed a small bowl of water in the run.

"Oh, it's great!" Mandy cried. Mr. Bell had made a square house up on little legs to keep it off the damp ground. He had also made a run with wire on the top and the bottom so Freddie wouldn't try to dig up the grass.

"Yes, it's perfect," Mrs. Santana agreed. "You'll

have to go around and thank him. Mr. Bell has worked really hard to make it so quickly."

Leanne gasped when she saw Freddie for the first time. "Oh, she's lovely. Can I hold her for a minute?"

"Just for a minute," Mrs. Santana said. She took the ferret from Danny and handed her to Leanne. Leanne held her carefully and stroked her soft fur.

"Be careful," Danny warned her as Freddie wriggled to get down.

"She's seen her new house and wants to explore it," Mandy said, chuckling.

Danny took the little creature from his sister's arms and popped her through the door of the cage. Leanne watched as Mandy placed the pipe in the run, then fastened the door safely.

"You mustn't ever open the door unless I'm here," Danny told his sister. "If she escapes again, we might never find her."

"I won't," Leanne promised.

Freddie seemed thrilled with her new home and ran around exploring. She rushed into the house, then out again. Next she popped into the pipe and disappeared, then, suddenly, her nose appeared out the other end. Everyone burst out laughing. Freddie really was the cutest little animal Mandy had ever seen.

# 5

# *Some News*

Mandy was still thinking about Freddie on Monday morning when the students lined up to go into their first class.

"Have you heard any news about Freddie's real owner?" Danny asked. He had spotted Mandy at the front of the line.

She shook her head. "No, have you?"

Danny shook his head as they filed into school. "No."

In class, Mrs. Todd told them more about the book fair.

"It's going to be a very important event," she said. "We badly need new books for the school library."

Mandy put up her hand. "Will there be any animal books, Mrs. Todd?"

"There'll be *all* kinds of books," her teacher told her, "but the school is only going to have enough money to buy *some* of them."

A groan went around the classroom.

"So . . ." Mrs. Todd went on, "Mrs. Garvie has decided we should try to raise some money to buy a lot more books." Mrs. Garvie was the principal. "We've had a meeting about it," she continued. "And we've decided to hold a school Fun Day in the playground."

"That sounds great," Mandy said to Gary Roberts, the boy sitting next to her.

Everyone started talking excitedly, and there was so much noise that Mrs. Todd had to clap her hands for silence. "All right, everyone," she called. "Now, we want everybody in grades three to six to help us."

"How?" Paul Stevens called out.

"Well," Mrs. Todd continued, "we need you all to think of ideas for money-raising booths. And you're to work in pairs. So will everyone choose a partner, please?"

"Will you be my partner?" Mandy turned and asked Danny, who was sitting behind her.

"Sure," Danny replied.

Mrs. Todd was still talking. "We're going to choose the twelve best ideas and we'll announce the winners on Friday," she said. "So start thinking, everyone."

Mandy loved village events. There had been fairs, dog shows, festivals — even a Bunny Bonanza — and now a school Fun Day. Her friends were already talking about things they could do. Someone said her mom might be able to make some cakes to sell.

Mandy sat at her desk and stared out the window. What on earth could she and Danny do to raise money?

"Tina Cunningham and I reckon we should get people to guess Blackie's weight," James told Mandy the following morning when they were on their way to school.

"That's a good idea," Mandy said with a sigh.

She had been thinking about a booth all the previous evening but hadn't come up with anything. She really hoped Danny had had a brainstorm.

"What are you and Danny going to do?" James asked. Mandy had already told him that she and Danny were going to be partners.

"I don't know," Mandy said, sighing again.

"Well, I'm sure you'll think of something." James spotted his classmate Tina coming up the road. "Hey, Tina!" he called. He ran toward her. "My dad says, if we get chosen, he'll get us a clipboard to write down everyone's entries."

Mandy met Danny just going into the classroom. "Hi, Danny. How's Freddie today?"

"Fine," Danny told her. "Come and see her later if you like."

"Thanks," Mandy said. "Have you had any ideas for our booth?"

Danny shrugged and shook his head. He sat down and started telling another friend about Freddie. Mandy went over to see the class gerbils, Terry and Gerry. Terry was asleep, rolled up in his bedding. She could just see his little nose peeping out from the straw. Gerry woke as the classroom filled up and started running around and around in his wheel. Mandy couldn't help smiling. Maybe she and Danny could suggest guessing how many times Gerry turned his wheel in five minutes? Then she sighed. That wouldn't be any good: Gerry usually slept most of the day, and it wouldn't be fair to wake him up on purpose.

Behind Mandy, everyone was talking about their ideas for Fun Day. Mrs. Todd came in and clapped her hands for silence.

"Right," she said. "Sit down, everyone. How are you all getting on with your booth ideas? Has anyone come up with anything yet?"

"Yes," several voices shouted.

Mandy didn't say anything. She felt miserable that she hadn't been able to think of an idea.

"Well," Mrs. Todd said, "let's hear some of them."

As the other children told the class about their schemes, Mandy felt sadder than ever. Unless she and Danny came up with an idea soon it would be too late.

"Don't worry, Mandy," Mrs. Todd said when she saw her worried face. "You'll think of something, I'm sure. You've got until Friday, remember."

Mandy bit her lip. Friday wasn't *that* far away, was it?

"But *everyone's* got an idea except us," Mandy said dismally as her mom picked her up from school that afternoon.

"Don't worry. Let's ask your dad," Dr. Emily said. "He's good at thinking up things like that."

But when Mandy got home and found her dad at the back of the clinic talking to Simon, he couldn't think of anything, either.

Dr. Adam went into the back room and returned with Mike Jordan's dog, Annie, in his arms. The little mongrel looked sleepy and a bit sick.

Mandy went to stroke her. "Maybe we could ask people to guess how many puppies Annie's going to have," she said, petting the little dog's head.

"I think she'll have them before your Fun Day," Dr. Adam told her. "In fact, I wouldn't be surprised if she had them tonight."

"Oh, that would be lovely!" Mandy said excitedly.

"I'll put her basket on the floor in one of the cupboards before I settle her down for the night," Simon said. "Dogs like to have a roof over their head when they're giving birth to puppies. It makes them feel safe and secure."

"When is Mr. Jordan coming back?" Mandy asked.

"In a few days," her dad replied. "It's a shame Annie couldn't have had her puppies in her own home, but she seems to be quite happy here at Animal Ark."

Mandy left Simon gently grooming Annie and went indoors for a snack. When she had finished, she rushed along to Danny's house to visit Freddie. James and Blackie were already there. Leanne was in their living room doing a jigsaw puzzle.

Danny was showing James the harness his mom had brought Freddie from Walton's pet shop.

Mandy's eyes shone with excitement. "I didn't know you could take ferrets for walks."

"Sure you can," Danny said as he fetched Freddie from her cage. He fixed the harness on carefully and attached a leash to a loop at the back. "Okay," he said, "let's go."

"Can I come?" Leanne appeared just as Danny put Freddie down. The ferret scampered over the back doorstep and out into the yard on the end of her leash. She didn't seem to mind wearing the harness at all.

"Not now, honey," Mrs. Santana called to Leanne from upstairs. "It's time for your bath."

Leanne stuck out her bottom lip and for a moment Mandy thought she was going to burst into tears. "It's not fair!" she whimpered, stamping her foot and running upstairs.

"Oh, dear," Mandy said. "It's a shame she couldn't come with us." She felt sorry for the little girl.

Lots of people stopped to admire Freddie as Mandy, James, Blackie, and Danny walked across the village square. Blackie thought it was great fun having another animal to walk with, and he kept stopping and sniffing the little creature. Freddie didn't seem to mind a bit — Mandy felt sure she must have been used to dogs before they had found her.

Mrs. Ponsonby was the first person they met. She was coming across the green with her fluffy, fat Pekingese dog, Pandora.

"Oh!" she exclaimed when she saw Freddie. "Is that a ferret?" The feather in her hat wobbled as she gazed down in disbelief. Pandora's tail wagged uncertainly as she smelled the strange little creature.

"It's Freddie," Mandy told her. "Isn't she lovely?"

Mrs. Ponsonby sniffed. "I'm not at all sure about that," she said, jerking Pandora's leash.

"Come along, darling. I don't think a ferret is a suitable friend for you."

Mrs. Ponsonby sailed away in the direction of the village hall.

The three friends walked Freddie around the village square, but then it began to rain so they hurried back home. By the time they got back they were all quite wet. Danny brought

Freddie indoors and dried her carefully with a towel.

"Ferrets can get bad colds," he told the others as they sat on the kitchen floor with Freddie playing around their feet. When Danny was sure the ferret was dry, he fetched a rubber ball. They all laughed as Freddie ran around pushing it in front of her.

"She's a good dribbler," James exclaimed with a chuckle.

"She'd make a great soccer player," Danny said. "You should see her pop the ball into her tunnel. She'd be a chief goal-scorer. . . . Watch." He went and fetched Freddie's pipe and put it down on the floor. Freddie pushed the ball across and into the tunnel. Then, suddenly, she and the ball popped out of the other end. They all laughed and Blackie barked. He wanted to join in the game as well.

Mandy suddenly had a great idea. If they could get several more pipes and make a maze with lots of ways in and out, they could pop Freddie in one end and people could win a prize if they guessed which hole she came out of.

Mandy turned to Danny and James, her eyes shining. "Danny, I've just had an idea!"

Danny looked puzzled. "You have?"

"Yes!" Mandy said excitedly.

"What could we give as prizes?" Danny asked, once Mandy had explained.

"You could ask your grandma to make a big batch of chocolate cookies," James suggested. "Then you could give one to everyone who guesses right."

"Great!" Mandy said. "Let's make a plan of the game to give to Mrs. Todd."

They put Freddie back into her house and Danny got some drawing paper and a pencil. Together, they sketched a plan of the tunnels.

Underneath, Mandy wrote out an explanation of the game. "I know," she said suddenly. "Let's call it 'Ferret Fun.' "

"That's great!" Danny told Mandy as she wrote the title at the top of the page.

When she had finished they sat back and

stared at the plan. The idea looked really good. But all the other ideas her friends had been talking about had sounded just as good. What chance did theirs have of getting picked for Fun Day?

# 6

# *Fingers Crossed*

Mandy could hardly sleep that night. She kept thinking about Ferret Fun and about Annie tucked up in her basket in the back room of the clinic. She made up her mind to get up especially early the next morning to go and see if the puppies had arrived.

There was a lovely surprise waiting for her in the morning when she ran down the stairs, still in her pajamas. Her dad had just come through from the clinic to see if she was awake.

"The puppies have arrived," he said. "Come and see, but don't make too much noise. Annie is feeling worn out, and we don't want to disturb her."

Mandy tiptoed after her dad. She gasped as she crouched down beside him to look at the newborn puppies. There were four of them — tiny pink squirming creatures nuzzling up to Annie. The little mongrel wagged her tail half-heartedly at Mandy and licked her hand when she stroked her.

"Oh, they're so *sweet*!" Mandy whispered. "You're such a clever girl, Annie."

Simon was standing by one of the benches, rubbing a fifth puppy gently with a towel to get its circulation going. "This one's not too well, I'm afraid," he said.

Mandy hurried over anxiously to look. Simon

was holding the tiniest puppy she had ever seen. It was much smaller than the others and lay still, not making any noise at all.

"The runt of the litter," Dr. Adam explained. "We'll be lucky if she survives, I'm afraid. Especially if the stronger ones don't let her feed."

Mandy's heart went out to the tiny, helpless creature as she touched it gently with her fingertip. "Couldn't we feed it with a bottle?" she asked. She knew Mike would be upset if one of Annie's puppies died.

"We might have to," Simon said. He gently put the puppy back with the others. "We'll keep an eye on her. Don't worry, Mandy."

When Mandy arrived at school, she and Danny handed in their sketch to Mrs. Todd before classes started.

There was a small frown on their teacher's face as she stared at the diagram and the explanation underneath. Then she looked at Mandy's and Danny's anxious faces staring up at her.

"Is Freddie your ferret?" she asked Danny.

Danny explained how they had discovered Freddie beneath Mandy's grandpa's shed.

"We don't know who she belongs to," Mandy said. Then she told Mrs. Todd about the notice at Animal Ark. She explained how they had asked nearly everyone in the village, but no one seemed to know where the ferret had come from.

"What if her owner turns up before Fun Day?" Mrs. Todd inquired.

Mandy bit her lip. "Oh, I didn't think of that," she said.

To her relief, Mrs. Todd smiled and said, "Well, we'll cross that bridge when we come to it, Mandy. For now, it seems a very good suggestion to me. I'll put it with the others for Mrs. Garvie to look at."

Mandy secretly kept her fingers crossed behind her back. She wanted Freddie's owner to show up but hoped it would be *after* Fun Day, not before.

"Maybe, if you asked your mom, you could bring Freddie to school to show the other chil-

dren," Mrs. Todd suggested to Danny. "As you are such a ferret expert, perhaps you could give us a little talk about her. We could have a ferret lesson."

"Okay," Danny said, with a grin. "When can I bring her?"

"Tomorrow, if you like," Mrs. Todd said. "You don't think being among so many people will frighten her, do you?"

Danny shook his head. "No, I don't think so. She seems to love being with people. I'll bring her toys — then everyone can see what fun she has playing with them."

"That will be lovely," Mrs. Todd said.

After school, Mandy rushed home to see Annie and her puppies. She had been thinking about them all day and had been hoping the tiny one was all right.

At the back of the clinic, Annie was in her basket, with the puppies sleeping contentedly by her side. Simon was sitting on a chair next to her. He was feeding the fifth puppy from a tiny bottle with a rubber nipple on the end made especially for baby animals.

Mandy watched as he tried to get the tiny creature to take some milk.

"I'm not having much luck, I'm afraid," he said sadly.

Mandy's heart sank. "We can't let her die, Simon."

Just then the phone rang. Simon handed the

puppy and the bottle to Mandy. "You try," he said. "See if you can make her take some."

Mandy cradled the puppy gently in her hand and pushed the nipple softly against its tiny muzzle. "Come on," she whispered, but the puppy turned its head away. Then Mandy remembered something she had seen her mom doing. She squeezed a few drops of milk onto a finger and held it close to the small dog's nose. The puppy's tiny pink tongue shot out and eagerly licked her finger. The next time Mandy offered the puppy the bottle, she took hold of the nipple and began to suck. By the time Simon returned, Mandy had managed to persuade the puppy to take nearly half of the milk.

"Well done," Simon said as he put the puppy back with the others. "She needs to be fed every four hours, so I'll try again after office hours. Your mom said she'd get up in the night to feed her."

"I could do that," Mandy said. She didn't think

she'd mind staying up *all* night if it meant the puppy's life would be saved.

Simon grinned. "Thanks, Mandy. Let's see how your mom manages first."

The next day, Dr. Emily appeared at the breakfast table looking rather sleepy. She had gotten up twice in the night to feed the puppy.

Mandy asked anxiously how the little creature was getting on.

Dr. Emily sighed. "She wouldn't take much milk. I'm afraid it's still touch and go."

When they got to school, Mandy and James waited for Danny by the gates. Mandy told James all about the sick puppy. "I know I'm not going to be able to think about anything else today," she confessed.

Danny soon came along, carrying Freddie in Grandma's shoe box. Mandy lifted the lid and peeped in. It cheered her up to see Freddie's bright eyes and to hear her little *tick-tick* sounds as the ferret gazed back at her.

In class, Mandy made sure the door was closed properly, then everyone sat in a circle on the floor as Danny took Freddie out of her box. Everyone drew in their breath as the ferret sat quietly in Danny's arms as he stroked her soft fur. Then they laughed as she climbed up his arm and sat on his shoulder, looking at them all with her bright eyes.

"Are you going to tell us something about her?" Mrs. Todd suggested once everyone had stroked Freddie and one or two people had held her.

"Lots of people have ferrets in America," Danny told everyone. "They're almost as popular as cats and dogs."

"Are there any wild ones?" Richard Tanner asked as he stroked Freddie's soft head. Danny took Freddie's ball from his pocket, and she began to push it around the floor. Everyone seemed amazed at how clever she was.

Danny shook his head in answer to Richard's question. "No. There are black-footed ferrets

that live in the wild, but they're not like tame ferrets," he told him.

"What other toys has she got?" someone else asked.

Danny told them about a little ladder his dad had made for Freddie's cage and a bell attached to some string tied to the top of the cage.

Then he told them all about his ferrets at home. Everyone laughed when he described how they loved having baths and playing with toys in the water.

"Does anyone know what a group of ferrets is called?" Mrs. Todd asked when Danny had finished.

Everyone shook their heads — even Danny, who knew more about ferrets than anyone else in the room.

"It's called a 'busyness,'" Mrs. Todd told them.

"That's a good name," Mandy said, laughing. She gazed at Freddie, who was running around exploring people's shoes and nibbling at their laces. "Because they are always busy."

When Freddie seemed to get tired, Danny put her back into the box. Mrs. Todd phoned Mrs. Santana to come and fetch her.

Mandy couldn't wait for school to end that day. Once Freddie had been taken home, her mind was only half on her lessons. There seemed to be so much else to think about. There was the little puppy struggling for survival at Animal Ark. Then there was Fun Day and the exciting book fair the following week. She wished Friday would come, when they would know if their booth had been chosen or not. But it still seemed such a long way off.

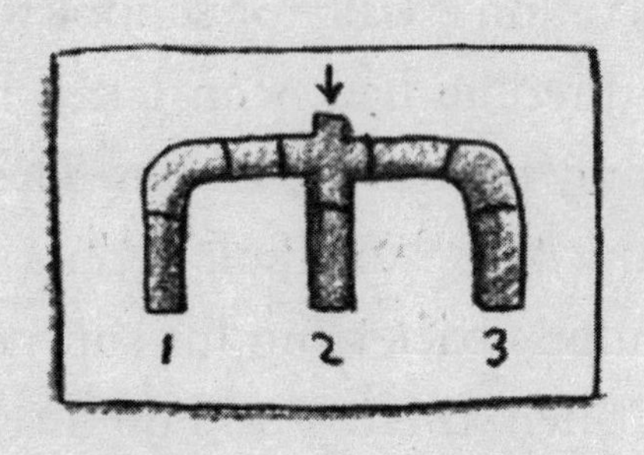


# 7

# *Making Plans*

Each day after school, Mandy and James went to play with Freddie and to help Danny clean out her cage. Then, after she had gone home and had a snack, Mandy would go and help Simon with Annie and her puppies.

"It looks like Freddie might never be claimed," she said to Simon one evening as she sat with the tiniest puppy on her lap. The little creature was at last beginning to thrive, and Mandy's mom and dad now had great hopes for her survival.

"She's a little fighter," Simon said to Mandy as she fed her with the bottle. "I reckon Mike will have five healthy puppies on his hands by the time he gets back from his trip."

"I'll miss them," Mandy said with a sigh. "And I'll miss Freddie — if we ever find her real owner."

"What will you do when your friend goes back to America?" Simon asked.

"I don't know." Mandy sighed again.

She helped settle Annie and her puppies down for the night and was just drinking her milk before bed when Dr. Adam came into the kitchen.

"I've just had a call from Mike Jordan," he told them. "He'll be back on Friday."

"Is he pleased about the puppies?" Mandy asked.

"Delighted," her dad told her. "He's only

sorry he wasn't here when they were born. And he's missed Annie terribly."

Mandy thought about Freddie. What about *her* owners? They must be worried sick about their pet. At least Mike knew Annie was being well looked after, but Freddie's owner wouldn't know *where* she was, or if she was being looked after at all!

On Friday morning, in assembly, Mrs. Garvie read out the names of the people whose ideas had been chosen for Fun Day. Mandy held her breath as she heard the principal say James's name. His game to guess Blackie's weight had been selected. She continued down the list. Mandy's heart began to sink. Mrs. Garvie had already announced eleven stalls and she hadn't mentioned Ferret Fun. But then she heard her name — "Mandy Hope and Danny Santana."

Mandy heaved a huge sigh of relief and her heart began to beat fast with excitement. They had a week to set up their game, as the Fun Day was to be held the following Saturday. They had to find pipes to make tunnels and something to make a fence out of, so Freddie couldn't escape. They also had to ask Grandma to make a very large batch of chocolate cookies and help her bake them.

It looked as though they were going to be very busy indeed.

After school, Mandy walked home with James and Danny. They chatted about Fun Day as they made their way to Danny's house. They were looking forward to playing with Freddie and telling her the good news about their stall before going home for their snack.

As they passed the end of the narrow footpath leading to Meadow Lane, Mandy saw Mike Jordan talking to a man outside his house. Mike had returned from his business trip and collected Annie and her puppies from the clinic.

"Come on," Mandy said to James and Danny. "Let's ask Mike what he thinks of the puppies."

They ran along the lane to see him.

There was a van parked in Mike's drive with SIDNEY BROWN — PLUMBER written on the side.

"Hello, you three," Mike exclaimed. "I'm glad I've seen you, Mandy. I wanted to thank you for helping with the pups."

"That's okay," Mandy assured him. "I loved doing it. Aren't they gorgeous?"

Mike grinned. "They're wonderful," he said.

"Is it okay if we go in and see them?" they asked.

"Of course," Mike said. "I'll be in in a minute."

They left him talking to the plumber and went inside Mike's cottage. Annie was in the living room, lying on the rug with the puppies around her. James and Danny were enchanted by them.

"Almost as much fun as ferrets," Danny said with a grin as one of the puppies managed to waddle toward him on tiny, unsteady legs.

"What's this about ferrets?" Mike came in from outside.

They explained quickly about Freddie, Fun Day, and their stall.

"Fun Day?" Mike asked. "What are you raising money for?"

They explained about the book fair.

"And we want to build a maze of tunnels for our stall," Mandy added.

"Well, I've got just the things you need, then," Mike said. He told them that the plumber had been installing a new bathroom while he had

been away. "And there's a pile of leftover pipes stacked in my yard," he continued. "They'll make a good maze for your ferret. Help yourselves to as many as you like."

"Wow, thanks," Danny said.

Outside, they examined the pile. They *were* just what they needed. Several of them had corner pieces, which they could fit together to make a kind of maze with several entrances.

"When should we come to get them?" Danny asked excitedly.

"Tomorrow, if it's all right with Mike," Mandy said. "I'll ask Grandpa if we can borrow his wheelbarrow."

"Good idea," Danny said.

Later, when Mandy got home for her supper, Dr. Emily came through from the clinic. Mandy was bursting to tell her the news about their stall and also about Mike and the pipes.

"That's great," Dr. Emily said when Mandy had told her everything.

"I'm going to ask Grandpa if we can borrow his wheelbarrow to take the pipes to Danny's house," Mandy said. She went out into the hall to phone him and explain why they needed them.

"Of course you can, love," Grandpa said. "No problem at all."

"Thanks, Grandpa," Mandy breathed. "See you tomorrow."

It was going to be great fun planning Freddie's maze of tunnels. She couldn't wait!

It was a lovely warm morning when Mandy, James, Blackie, and Danny met on the village square and made their way to Lilac Cottage. When they got there, Grandpa was already in the garden hoeing his vegetable patch. The wheelbarrow was waiting for them.

"What are you going to give as prizes at this booth of yours?" Grandpa asked.

Mandy told him about Grandma's chocolate cookies. "Do you think she'll make them for us?" she asked anxiously.

"I'm sure she will," Grandpa said with a smile. "She's indoors. Go on in and ask her."

They all ran inside. Grandma was sitting at the kitchen table reading the *Walton Gazette.* She looked up as they burst in.

"Hello, you three! I've just been reading about you in the paper."

"Us!" Danny exclaimed. He peered over Grandma's shoulder.

"Yes." She pointed to a big advertisement. "Look."

*Welford Village Primary School*
FUN DAY
*Welford Village School*
*Saturday, 2 P.M.*
*Tortoise Walk, Guess the Dog's Weight,*
*Egg Stall, Skittles, Ferret Fun,*
*and lots, lots more . . .*
*Entrance 50 pence*
BRING THE WHOLE FAMILY

"It's *Blackie's* weight people have got to guess," James explained.

Grandma's eyes twinkled. "I thought it might be."

"And Freddie is the ferret," Mandy told her.

Grandma laughed and gave her a quick hug. "I guessed that, too, love. You *are* going to be busy."

Mandy asked her grandma if she might have time to bake some cookies for them to give as prizes.

"I remember how good they are," Danny piped up. "*Everyone* will want to win one."

Grandma laughed and gave him a hug as well. "Well, thank you, Danny," she said. "I'll certainly do my best."

They said good-bye to Grandma and Grandpa and trundled the wheelbarrow along to Meadow Lane to collect the pipes.

Mandy knocked on Mike's door to tell him they had arrived. As he opened it, Annie ran out to say hello to everybody. Then she and Blackie began chasing each other around the yard. She was certainly her old self again.

The puppies appeared at the front door next, waddling to find where their mom had gone. Mandy and Mike scooped them up gently before they could tumble down the steps and hurt themselves, and they carried them back indoors. Mandy was delighted to see the little one keeping up with the others.

"I've called her Mandy in your honor," Mike told her. "Especially since you helped look after her when she was first born."

Mandy was thrilled. "Oh, thanks, Mike!" she said.

"Are you coming to our Fun Day?" James asked Mike as they went back outside to help sort out the pipes and load them onto the wheelbarrow.

"You bet," Mike said. His eyes lit up when he heard about Grandma's cookies. "I'll be the first one at the ferret booth, then," he said with a grin.

"What are you giving as a prize to whoever guesses Blackie's weight?" Danny asked James.

"Mom said she'd buy a big box of fudge,"

James told him as he loaded the last pipe onto the wheelbarrow.

"Sounds good to me," Mike said as he opened the gate so they could wheel the wheelbarrow through. "See you on Saturday, then."

"Thanks." Mandy waved as they set off to Danny's house.

When they had washed the pipes they stood looking at them thoughtfully. Then Mandy knelt down and began putting them together.

Soon they had made an E shape that had an extra entrance so they could pop Freddie into the maze.

Mandy sat back on her heels looking pleased. "Great," she said. She looked at Danny. "Maybe we'd better let Freddie practice before Saturday."

Danny went to fetch Freddie from her cage. She had really settled down in her new home now and looked well fed and happy. Her coat was glossy and her eyes were bright as beads.

"She's lovely," Mandy said as Danny gave

Freddie to her. She stroked the ferret gently, then showed her the maze of tunnels, putting her down in front of the top entrance. Freddie sniffed around for a moment or two, then disappeared inside.

"Which one do you think she'll come out of?" Mandy whispered.

"The first one," James said.

"No, the second," Danny said.

"I bet it'll be the third." Mrs. Santana had come into the yard and was crouching down beside them.

Then they shouted with delight as Freddie popped her head out of tunnel number two.

Danny jumped up and down and clapped his hands. "I won! I won!"

Everyone laughed as he popped Freddie back into the tunnel entrance. This time she came out of number one.

"Maybe you should paint the numbers on the pipes," his mom suggested.

"And you'll need a fence around them, to

make sure Freddie doesn't try to run off," James said.

"Why don't you ask Mr. Bell if he's got some planks of wood you could borrow?" Mrs. Santana said. "He told me he's got some carrots for me, so you could go to get them and ask him then."

By the time they had finished painting the numbers on the tunnels, it was almost lunchtime. Before Mandy and James went home, they popped in to see Mr. Bell. He was in his garden shed.

"Fun Day?" he said with a frown when they told him about Freddie and her tunnels.

"We need to raise money for some new books for school," Mandy explained.

"Books?" Mr. Bell frowned again. "Oh . . . well, books are a good idea. I'll see if I can find you some planks of wood to fence in that ferret of yours. Mind you, I want them back."

"Oh, thank you, Mr. Bell," Mandy said. "We'll let you have a free try at our booth. You might win one of Grandma's chocolate chip cookies."

A smile spread slowly over the old man's face. "I'm very fond of your grandma's baking," he said, "so I might even have more than one try. I'll pay for the others, of course," he added quickly.

"All right, then." Mandy smiled.

"Thanks, Mr. Bell," they called again as they made their way back to Danny's house.

Mandy said good-bye to the Santanas and James and Blackie as they went their separate ways home for lunch. Although there was still a week to go before Fun Day, she was already very excited. Freddie's booth had turned out to be great, and she was sure it would make lots of money for the book fair. She just couldn't wait for next Saturday to come. But suppose someone did turn up and take Freddie away — what would they do then?

# 8

# *Leanne's Secret*

Mandy and Danny were practicing setting up the tunnels again. They wanted the stall to be just right for Fun Day, and Freddie seemed to be having great fun playing in them.

"She really loves them," Danny commented as they watched the ferret popping in and out of the maze. "I bet our stall is going to be really popular and raise lots of money."

"I hope so," Mandy said. She hoped *everyone* would raise lots of money and all the shelves in the school library would be full of new books.

Mrs. Santana came out with a drink of lemonade for them both.

"How's Leanne?" Mandy asked when she had said thank you. Leanne was in bed with a bad cold.

"She's still under the weather," Mrs. Santana said. "You can go up and see her if you like."

Mandy climbed the stairs to Leanne's room. The little girl was sitting up in bed. She had a red nose and looked very unhappy.

Mandy sat down on the end of her bed, feeling sorry for Leanne. "I hope you're better before Saturday," she said, trying to cheer the little girl up.

"Mom says I won't be able to go if I'm not better," Leanne grumbled. "But I don't care."

"Oh, dear. You'll miss all the fun," Mandy exclaimed.

Leanne shrugged and then, sniffing, she lay down and buried her face in the pillow. Mandy sighed. She wished she *could* do something to cheer Danny's sister up. She tried to get Leanne to talk, but the little girl wouldn't answer. She just lay there with her eyes shut tight. Mandy gave up and went back downstairs.

"Don't worry, Mandy," Mrs. Santana said. "She's feeling sorry for herself. I'm sure she'll cheer up soon."

"I hope so," Mandy said. She didn't like the thought of Leanne missing all the events at the Fun Day.

Saturday arrived and still no one had turned up to claim Freddie. Mandy was glad but also a bit anxious. Danny would be going back to America in a few weeks' time — and then what?

"We'll just have to find another home for her, love," Dr. Emily said at breakfast on Fun Day morning. "I'll contact the vet in Walton to see if she knows anyone who keeps ferrets and might like another one."

"That's a good idea." Mandy finished the last of her cereal, gulped down her glass of milk, and rushed from the table. "I've got to go to Danny's, then to Mr. Bell's, along to school, then to Grandma's, and then back to fetch Freddie, then . . ." she said all in one breath.

Her mom laughed. "Slow down, Mandy. There's plenty of time. The Fun Day doesn't start until two o'clock."

Mandy was already halfway out the door. "I know, but there's so much to do!"

First she went to Lilac Cottage to collect Grandpa's wheelbarrow. They were going to use it to take the pipes to the school playground.

Grandpa had gone shopping with Grandma, but he had left the wheelbarrow outside the front gate for Mandy. She and Danny had helped Grandma make a huge batch of cookies, which Mandy would collect later.

She wheeled the wheelbarrow quickly along to Danny's house. She parked it on the path and knocked on the front door.

When Danny opened it, she could see by his face that something was wrong.

"It's Freddie." Danny looked as if he was about to burst into tears. "I can't find her anywhere."

Mandy's hand flew to her mouth. "Oh, no! How did she escape?"

Danny shrugged. "The cage door was open. I guess I didn't close it properly when I fed her last night."

Mandy, Danny, and his parents searched everywhere for Freddie, but she was nowhere to be found. They went up and down the road, into the yard of the Fox and Goose, and along to the other houses in the row. They peered under sheds, into greenhouses, searched behind fences and inside garages. There was no sign of the ferret. And although they asked every person they came across, no one had seen her anywhere.

"It's no good," Danny said miserably when they all met up again back at his house. "She's gone."

Mandy swallowed back tears. "Have you looked indoors?"

"Yes, but we can look again, I guess," Danny's dad said. "She might be curled up somewhere we forgot to search."

They hunted all over the house, but there was no sign of Freddie.

"Maybe she didn't want to be in Fun Day after all," Danny said unhappily as they discussed what to do next.

"Perhaps you could borrow someone else's ferret?" Mrs. Santana suggested. "They all like playing in tunnels."

But Mandy shook her head. "We don't know anyone else who's got one."

They went into the yard again to take another look, but Mandy stayed behind, racking her brains for ideas. She felt so sad. She sat on the bottom stair and couldn't help the tears running down her cheeks. Everything was ruined. And poor Freddie! She could be in danger with no one to look after her. Mandy had been so excited, and now things were going horribly wrong.

She was rubbing her eyes with a tissue when she heard a noise at the top of the stairs. Mandy looked up and saw Leanne standing at the top, staring down at her.

"Hi, Leanne," Mandy said. "*You* haven't seen Freddie, have you?"

Leanne was leaning against the wall at the top of the stairs, fiddling with the ribbon on her nightdress. "No," she said, shaking her head.

"She's managed to get out of her cage," Mandy continued. "We can't find her anywhere, and we don't know what we're going to do."

Leanne shuffled her feet. "Do you want to come up to see my bedroom?" she asked in a small voice.

"I've seen it," Mandy reminded her. "And I should really be out hunting for Freddie." She stood up. "Are you coming to Fun Day?"

Leanne wasn't looking at her. "Don't know," she said in a half whisper.

"Well, anyway, it won't be so much fun without our booth," Mandy said. She could hardly bear to think about it.

She was about to go back out into the yard when Leanne called her. "Please come up, Mandy," she insisted.

Mandy sighed. She should be out helping to hunt for Freddie, but the little girl sounded so miserable that she reluctantly agreed.

"Okay," she said, and climbed the stairs. Leanne had already disappeared back into her bedroom, so Mandy followed her. She was surprised to see the little girl curled up in bed, the quilt drawn up to her chin.

Leanne lay quiet as a mouse as Mandy went over and sat on the end of the bed. "I'm sorry you're not . . ." she began. Then, to her surprise, a tiny head peeped out from under the corner of the pillow. Mandy couldn't help giving a little squeal of surprise to see Freddie's little pink nose and bright eyes peering at her.

"Oh, Leanne! You've had her all the time!" she gasped. Then she collapsed into chuckles. Freddie looked so cute in bed with Leanne. "What's your mom going to say?" she said. "And Danny!"

Leanne gave a little smile, then her face fell and she started to cry. "I'm sorry, I only wanted to play with her for a little while. I was going to put her back, but Danny started yelling that she'd escaped and I was scared."

"Oh, *dear*!" Mandy sighed.

"I'm sorry," Leanne wailed again. "But everyone's got a pet and I don't."

Mandy went and picked Freddie up. "That's not true, Leanne," she said gently as she stroked Freddie's fur. "*I* don't have a pet of my own, but I do like sharing other people's. It's almost as good."

"Don't tell Danny. Please, Mandy," Leanne begged her. "He'll be so mad at me."

Mandy sat down with Freddie on her lap. "Okay," she said. "It can be our secret. But don't *ever* take Freddie out of her cage without Danny there again, will you?"

Leanne shook her head. "I won't, I promise."

Then Mandy had an idea. "Would you like to help out with our booth today — if your mom says it's all right?"

A bright smile lit up Leanne's face. "Oh, yes, *please*!" She threw back the covers and jumped out of bed. "I do feel much better."

Mandy gave the little girl a hug. "I'd better tell everyone I've found Freddie, hadn't I?"

Leanne nodded.

Mandy carried Freddie down the stairs and called out to the others. "It's okay, I've found her!"

They all came running indoors.

"Where was she?" Danny looked very relieved.

"Hiding in Leanne's room," Mandy said.

Luckily, Danny was so pleased to see the ferret that he didn't ask any more questions. Mandy had a feeling Mrs. Santana had guessed Leanne had taken her, because she went upstairs right away to talk to her. When they came down a little later, Leanne was dressed and ready to go out.

"My cold's much better," she said, beaming at Danny and Mr. Santana. "And Mom says I can help you."

"Help us?" Danny frowned.

"Yes," Mandy said quickly, winking at him. "We need someone to look after the cookies."

"Do we?" Danny said. "Oh, yes, I guess we do."

After that, there was so much to do that the morning sped by in a whirl. They groomed Freddie so she would look really pretty, then loaded the wheelbarrow and trundled it down to the school playground. It was already buzzing with activity.

Mrs. Todd was setting up a knickknack booth, and Mrs. Garvie was showing everyone where their booths were going to be. Mr. and Mrs. Ransley, who ran the Cub Scouts, had brought one of their tents. They were busy putting it up in the corner of the field next to the playground. All the booth-holders would take the competition results along to the tent and Reverend Hadcroft would announce them at the end of the day.

Mandy and Danny set up the tunnels for Freddie, then hurried back to collect the planks from Mr. Bell. He had stacked them against his shed ready for collection. By the time they had carted them to the school, set them up in a square around the maze, then collected the big tin of delicious-looking cookies from Grandma, it was almost time for the fun to begin. People were already arriving as Mandy and Danny went to do the last job of all — fetching Freddie.

They had borrowed a pet carrier from the clinic, and Freddie was soon safely inside. They carried her carefully back along the street toward the school. She seemed to know something unusual was happening and ran around the cage, making excited little *tick-tick* noises.

As they made their way back, Mandy spotted James and Tina bringing Blackie across the village square. Blackie looked very handsome — James had brushed him until his coat shone. He even had a red ribbon around his neck. He had a notice attached to him that said GUESS MY WEIGHT. Tina carried the pen and clipboard, where people would write down their guesses, and a huge box of fudge to present to the winner. Mandy waved. James and Tina waved back and hurried to take their place at school.

Mandy noticed her mom and dad arriving with Simon, and Mrs. Ponsonby with Pandora, together with Mrs. Forsyth from the riding stables. Mr. and Mrs. Santana were already there with Leanne. Mandy's heart drummed with excitement when she saw so many people turning up. There were lots of people she knew and some she didn't. People seemed to be coming from all over the place to help raise funds for the school library.

This was going to be the best day Welford had ever known!

# 9

# *Good News for Freddie*

As soon as Mrs. Garvie had declared Fun Day open, people started to crowd around Mandy and Danny's stall. There were so many that Mandy had to ask them to stand back. Otherwise, no one could see which tunnel Freddie popped out of.

It wasn't long before the purse they were

putting their money in was feeling really heavy. After each try, Mandy carefully wrote down the number of correct guesses, while Leanne stood guarding the cookie tin. The sun was quite hot, and Mandy hoped the chocolate wouldn't melt before the end of the day.

"Umm, those cookies look nice," a little boy said as he stood talking to Danny's sister. He looked about Leanne's age, but Mandy didn't recognize him.

"Mandy's grandma made them," the little girl told him. "You can win one if you guess which tunnel Freddie is going to come out of."

The little boy nodded in the direction of the other games.

"My dad's over there," he told her. "He said he'll come and have a try at your booth next, but I wanted to see the ferret. Is it yours?" he asked Leanne.

Leanne shook her head. "She's my brother's."

"*She?*" the boy squealed. "Freddie's a funny name for a girl!" They all laughed.

"We called her Freddie before we knew she was a girl," Mandy explained. "It seemed to suit her, so we didn't want to change it. We didn't think she'd mind."

"Oh." The little boy laughed.

Just then, his dad came across to look at the stall. "Oh, there you are, Timmy." Then he spotted Freddie. "This is a nice ferret." He turned to Mandy and Danny. "Is it yours?"

"Well, she's not actually Danny's," Mandy

told him. "She's a stray. We're just looking after her until she's claimed."

"A stray?" Timmy's dad frowned. He went on staring at Freddie as she popped out of tunnel number three and everyone cheered. Leanne handed over a cookie to someone who had guessed correctly.

"Did *you* find her, then?" Timmy's dad asked.

"Yes." Mandy explained about Freddie hiding beneath Grandpa's shed.

"We've got ferrets," Timmy told them.

"*And* we lost one a few weeks ago," his dad added thoughtfully. "One just like this. Can I pick her up?"

"Yes, of course," Mandy said.

Timmy's dad picked Freddie up and stroked her. "Mine was called Pixie," he told them. "She escaped when I was cleaning out her cage."

"Oh." Mandy gazed at him. "Do you live in Welford?"

Timmy's dad shook his head. "No, just outside. We've only been there a few months. The move from our old house upset the ferrets a bit." He still looked thoughtful. "You know, this one really looks just like Pixie."

"We've been trying to find her owner," Danny told him. "We've asked everyone."

"So have my mom and dad," Mandy added. "They've asked all the people who have come into their clinic, but no one knew anything about a lost ferret."

"Clinic?" Timmy's dad looked puzzled.

"Yes." Dr. Adam had just come to have a try at the booth. He had heard what the man said and introduced himself. "My wife and I are the vets here in Welford. Freddie was in pretty poor condition when they found her. We thought she'd been lost for some time."

"Well, she looks great now," Timmy's dad said. He shook Dr. Adam's hand. "I'm Dave Wright. I've got six ferrets and if this *is* Pixie, I reared her from a kitten. She was my favorite, as she was so friendly." He put Freddie back

down and she scampered into one of the tunnels.

"Six ferrets!" Mandy exclaimed. "Wow!"

"Two are mine," Timmy said. He pulled at his dad's arm. "Can we take her home, Dad?"

"We'll have to make sure she's ours first," his dad told him.

"Could you identify Pixie?" Dr. Adam asked him.

Mr. Wright looked thoughtful for a minute. "Well, she had a little white mark under her tummy," he told them.

"So has Freddie!" Mandy said excitedly. "You remember, Dad. We saw it when you were examining her."

"That's right," Dr. Adam said. He smiled at Timmy. "Well, Timmy, it looks like your dad's found his missing ferret."

Mr. Wright grinned broadly. "Well, well. That's really great. I thought I'd never see her again."

"Please, may we keep her until the end of the show?" Mandy asked anxiously. She felt a bit sad that they would have to say good-bye to Freddie, although she was delighted her real owner had turned up at last.

"No problem," Mr. Wright said. "I'll pick her up at the end of the day. Do you want to look around the other booths?" he asked Timmy.

"Can Leanne come as well?" Timmy asked.

"Of course she can," his dad said, "as long as she tells her mom and dad."

Mandy smiled to herself. It hadn't taken Leanne and Timmy long to become friends.

Danny found Mrs. Santana, who said it was fine for Leanne to go with Timmy and his dad for a little while.

"What about looking after the cookies?" Leanne asked Mandy.

"Oh, I'm sure we can manage for a while," Mandy said. "You go and have some fun."

"Thanks, Mandy!" Leanne ran off with Timmy, and Mandy watched them go. It was really nice to see the little girl so happy. She turned back to the others. "Are you going to have a try at our booth, Dad?"

"Of course." Dr. Adam handed over his fifty cents as Danny popped Freddie into the entrance tunnel.

"You're allowed to have three guesses," Mandy told him. They all burst out laughing when her dad was wrong each time.

"No cookies for you, I'm afraid, Dad," Mandy said.

A little while later, Leanne came back and helped Danny while Mandy went to visit the other stalls. She tried to guess Blackie's weight, threw three balls and knocked five pins down, and managed to pick up two empty eggshells from the egg stall.

Every stall was buzzing with people, and it looked as if lots of money would be raised. Tina and James had a long list of people who had tried to guess Blackie's weight. Blackie was having a lovely time, as everyone who had a try fussed over him at the same time. Sarah and Jill had brought Jill's tortoise, Toto, safely tucked in a box with some straw, so people could look at him and try to guess how slowly he would cross the booth. There was a crowd around Carrie and Peter's bowling alley, waiting to throw the balls and knock them down.

"I was quite a champion at bowling when I was a boy," Grandpa told Mandy as he managed to scatter all the pins in one try.

She laughed and gave him a hug. "You're a champion at most things, Grandpa." Then she told him about Mr. Wright.

"That's grand, love. Freddie will be pleased to be back with her ferret friends," he said.

Then Mandy spotted Mike Jordan. She ran across to ask him how Annie and her puppies were getting on. To her surprise, Mike was also running a competition.

"I thought I'd help the school raise some money," he told her. He was holding a clipboard with a photograph of Annie's tiny puppy on it. "I'm asking people to guess her name," he said. "And I'm giving a book token as a prize. That's if anyone gets it right," he added with a grin. "If not, I'll present the book token to the school and they can use it to buy a book at the fair."

"Oh!" Mandy gave a huge smile. "But I *know* what her name is already."

Mike grinned at her. "You won't give the game away, will you?"

"Of course not," she told him. She had been so busy with plans for Fun Day she had forgotten to tell anyone that Mike had named the puppy after her.

The rest of the afternoon flew past, and when the church clock struck half past five Mrs. Garvie said it was time to close all the booths. Mandy thought *everyone* must have had a try at their booth, because all the cookies were gone and Freddie was tired out. She had gone into one of the tunnels and fallen fast asleep.

Mr. Bell won the competition to guess Blackie's weight — twenty-one pounds. Mr. Bell couldn't hide a great big grin when he went to collect his prize.

When all the winners had been announced,

Mrs. Garvie called out the grand total of money that had been raised.

"Two hundred and twenty-six pounds," she called, as everyone clapped and cheered again.

Mandy turned to her mom, her eyes shining. "That will buy loads of books," she said excitedly.

Dr. Emily grinned. "It certainly will."

When it was time to go, Mr. Wright came to get Freddie. Dr. Adam had lent him the pet carrier, and he promised to return it when Timmy came to Welford to play with Leanne.

" 'Bye, Freddie." Mandy gave the little ferret one last cuddle. She felt tears spring to her eyes. She would miss her like anything.

Danny and James and Leanne also gave Freddie a final cuddle.

"Thanks for looking after her," Mr. Wright said as he put Freddie gently into the carrier. "Perhaps you'd like to come and see my other ferrets sometime."

"We'd love to. Wouldn't we, Danny?" Mandy said.

"Sure," Danny said. "I'll ask Mom to bring us over before we go back to the States."

Mr. Wright shook hands and thanked Mandy, Danny, and James, and Dr. Adam and Dr. Emily, and Grandma and Grandpa, *and* Mr. Bell. They had all helped to make Freddie's stay in Welford such a happy one.

Mandy felt sad as she watched Mr. Wright and Timmy put Freddie into their car and drive away. She gave a big sigh. She was glad Freddie was back with her real owners but knew she would really miss her.

# 10

## *The Book Fair*

When the day of the book fair arrived, Dr. Emily gave Mandy five pounds to buy herself some books to bring home.

"That's for working so hard for the Fun Day," she explained.

Mandy's eyes shone as she gave her mom a big hug. "Thanks, Mom."

When she arrived at school, a big white van was parked outside. Two men were unloading huge metal containers full of books and wheeling them inside on a trolley. Mrs. Todd and James's teacher, Mrs. Black, were waiting in the hall. They had set up long tables to put the books on. They had also put up some screens with posters advertising all sorts of books.

After assembly, Mrs. Garvie had an announcement to make.

"The book fair will take place during break and at lunchtime," she told everyone. "And your teachers will also be there, choosing which books to buy for the school."

"Are you going to buy any for yourself?" Mandy whispered to Danny, who was sitting, cross-legged, on the floor next to her.

"I'm going to get one for Leanne," Danny said a bit guiltily. "I'd like to make up for being so grumpy with her. I hadn't realized she was so unhappy."

"Is she still unhappy, then?" Mandy asked.

Danny shook his head. "No, she's okay now

that she's got Timmy as a friend, but I thought she'd like a book anyway."

Mandy smiled. "I'm sure she'd love one, Danny."

"And don't forget," Mrs. Garvie went on, "that for every book you buy to take home, the school is given a small amount of the money. *That* will help us buy even more books for the library."

Mandy could hardly concentrate on her lessons, she was thinking so much about the book fair. When break came, she rushed into the hall. It was already crowded with pupils from other classes. She soon found James — he had brought some money to school as well.

"You can buy some of them at a special low price," Mrs. Black told Mandy as she looked through some of the paperback books. There was one about the adventures of a fox and another about dogs. At their special price, she had enough money to buy them both!

"May I have these two, please?" she asked, holding out her money.

"Of course you can, Mandy." Mrs. Black put the books into a paper bag.

James was still deciding what to choose so Mandy went to find Danny. He was looking at the picture books, trying to find one for his sister.

They looked through them together and finally found a book about kittens they thought Leanne would like. Mandy showed Danny the books she had bought, then she helped him to choose one for himself.

Everyone was crowding around the tables. Mandy went across to look at the books the teachers had bought for the library with the money raised on Fun Day. There were two huge piles of them — lots of picture books for the younger children, a couple of big encyclopedias and a stack of storybooks for the older students. They all looked very exciting and Mandy couldn't wait to borrow some.

When break was over, Mrs. Todd told them they would have another chance to look at the books during their lunch break. Parents and friends had been invited to come along to buy books as well, and the school was expecting lots of people to turn up.

Before the children went back to their classrooms, Mrs. Garvie had a message for them.

"I want to say thank you for working so hard to raise this money," she told everyone. "Thanks to you, our library shelves are almost full." Then she looked at Mandy and Danny. "We've decided to give a small prize to the booth that raised the most money," she said. "And I'm pleased to say it was Mandy Hope and Danny Santana's Ferret Fun."

Mandy and Danny both gasped with surprise. They had no idea their stall had raised more money than any of the others.

"Would you both like to come forward, please?" Mrs. Garvie called.

Everyone clapped as Mandy and Danny went across to where the principal was standing. "Come back at lunchtime and you can each choose a book to take home," she said.

Mandy's and Danny's eyes were shining as they thanked her.

James caught up with them as they filed back to their classrooms. "Well done, you two," he said. "That's great."

"You'll have to help us decide," Mandy said, "because *you* helped with Freddie, too."

When lunchtime came, they all hurried back to the book fair. Danny chose a book about England as his prize. "It will remind me of Welford when I get back home," he said.

James helped Mandy decide. Finally she came across a book about ferrets and chose that one. "You can borrow it anytime you like," she said to James.

Mandy opened the book. On the first page there was a picture of a honey-colored ferret that looked just like Freddie.

"If it hadn't been for Freddie, we would never have raised so much money," she said, with a smile.

Mandy gazed at the bright eyes of the little

creature in the picture. Although she missed Freddie, she knew the ferret was pleased to be back in her real home. Mr. Wright had phoned to say she had settled down and was none the worse for her adventure.

Mandy gave a little sigh of happiness. There was no doubt about it: looking after Freddie really had been great fun!